GET READY...GET SET...READ!

NIGHT LIGHT

by
Foster & Erickson

Illustrations by
Kerri Gifford

BARRON'S

Whiptail was telling a tale
at camp one night.

"Stop the tall tales,"
said Gail.
"They give me a fright."

"Okay, Gail," said Whiptail.
"Let's go to Blackshale Trail,

and find the raccoon
who lives near the dunes."

"All right!" said Dwight.
"This is keen," said Dean.
"Let's go!" said Colleen.

"Oh no!" said Gail
and she turned pale.

"Hold on to me,"
said Whiptail.
"I have a night light.

It's black out tonight
so hold on tight."

So Dwight, Dean, Dale,
Colleen and Gail,

all went with Whiptail
down Blackshale Trail.

"Did you hear that?"
wailed Gail.
And she turned pale.

"It's just a loon,
crooning a tune.
Let's keep going."

"All right!" said Dwight.
"This is keen," said Dean.
"Let's go!" said Colleen.

"Oh no!" said Gail
and she turned pale.

"What's that?" asked Gail.
"It looks quite mean."

"It's a tree, an old evergreen.
Let's keep going."

"What's that?" asked Gail,
"over there by the dune."

"Oh Gail, can't you see?
It is the raccoon."

"All right," said Gail.
"We've seen him.
Now let's go back."

Just then,
everything went black.

"Oh no!" wailed Whiptail,
"there goes my light."

"Stop the tall tales,"
said Gail,
"and turn it up bright."

23

"He can't," said Dale,
"the light is out for tonight."

"They are right," said Dwight,
"there is no more light."

"But this night is so black

we might never get back!"

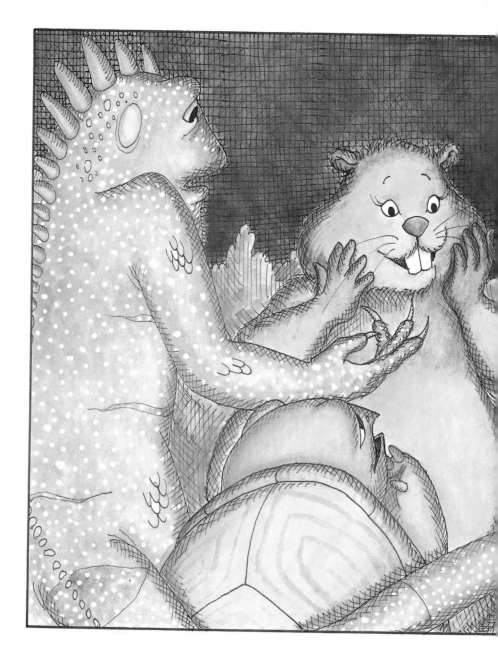

"We'll be all right
with our new night light,"
said Colleen.

"For very soon,
we can find our way back. . .

by the light of the moon."

DEAR PARENTS AND EDUCATORS:

Welcome to *Get Ready...Get Set...Read!*

We've created these books to introduce children to the magic of reading.

Each story in the series is built around one or two word families. For example, *A Mop for Pop* uses the OP word family. Letters and letter blends are added to OP to form words such as TOP, LOP, and STOP.

This *Bring-It-All-Together* book serves as a reading review. When your children have finished *Whiptail of Blackshale Trail, Colleen and the Bean, Dwight and the Trilobite, The Old Man at the Moat,* and *By the Light of the Moon,* it is time to have them read this book. *Night Light* uses some of the characters and most of the words introduced in the fourth set of five *Get Ready...Get Set...Read!* stories. (Each set in the series will be followed by two review books.)

Bring-It-All-Together books provide:
• much needed vocabulary repetition for developing fluency.
• longer stories for increasing reading attention spans.
• new stories with familiar characters for motivating young readers.

We have created these *Bring-It-All-Together* books to help develop confidence and competence in your young reader. We wish you much success in your reading adventures.

Kelli C. Foster, Ph.D.   Gina Clegg Erickson, MA
Educational Psychologist   Reading Specialist

All inquiries should be addressed to:
Barron's Educational Series, Inc.
250 Wireless Boulevard, Hauppauge, NY 11788

International Standard Book Number 0-8120-9335-6
Library of Congress Catalog Card Number: 95-45820

Library of Congress Cataloging-in-Publication Data
Foster, Kelli C.
    Night light / by Foster & Erickson ; illustrations by Kerri Gifford.
        p.   cm. — (Get ready— get set— read!)
        Summary; Campers have to use the light of the moon when their flashlight burns out.
        ISBN 0-8120-9335-6
        (1. Camps—Fiction. 2. Stories in rhyme.) I. Erickson, Gina Clegg.
    II. Gifford, Kerri, ill. III. Title. IV. Series: Erickson, Gina Clegg. Get ready— get set— read!
    PZ8.3.F813Ni · 1996
    (E)—dc20   95-45820
                                                                   CIP
                                                                   AC

PRINTED IN HONG KONG
6789   9927   987654321

There are five sets of books in the

Series. Each set consists of five **FIRST BOOKS** and two **BRING-IT-ALL-TOGETHER BOOKS**.

SET 1

is the first set your children should read.
The word families are selected from the short vowel sounds:
at, **ed**, **ish** and **im**, **op**, **ug**.

SET 2

provides more practice
with short vowel sounds:
an and **and**, **et**, **ip**, **og**, **ub**.

SET 3

focuses on
long vowel sounds:
ake, **eep**, **ide** and **ine**, **oke** and **ose**, **ue** and **ute**.

SET 4

introduces the idea that the word family sounds
can be spelled two different ways:
ale/ail, **een/ean**, **ight/ite**, **ote/oat**, **oon/une**.

SET 5

acquaints children with word families that
do not follow the rules for long and short vowel sounds:
all, **ound**, **y**, **ow**, **ew**.